Sing a song of sixpence

Illustrated by Linda Edwards

Designed by Amanda Barlow
Edited by Jenny Tyler
Music arranged by Eileen O'Brien

Sing a song of sixpence,
A pocket full of rye;
Four and twenty blackbirds
Baked in a pie.

When the pie was opened
The birds began to sing,
Wasn't that a dainty dish
To set before the King?

The King was in his counting house, Counting out his money;

The Queen was in the parlour,
Eating bread and honey;

The maid was in the garden,
Hanging out the clothes,
When down came a blackbird
And pecked off her nose!